What lies at the end of the rainbow? Is there merely a pot of gold, or might there be another sort of treasure — a treasure that may be reached by anyone willing to undertake the journey?

For if you follow the rainbow to its end and look into its shimmering colors, you will find a great oak tree with a door at the base of the trunk.

If you open the door and step inside, you will meet Mrs. Murgatroyd™, the wise woman who lives there. In her paint pots she collects all the colors of the rainbow.

And if you take up a paintbrush and picture whatever is in your heart, you will discover a treasure far more valuable than gold.

Tanya and the Green-Eyed Monster

Series concept by Ayman Sawaf and Kevin Ryerson
Developed from actual case histories by art therapist Liz Farrington
Copyright ©1993 by Enchanté Publishing
MRS. MURGATROYD character copyright ©1993 by Enchanté
MRS. MURGATROYD is a trademark of Enchanté
Series format and design by Jaclyne Scardova
Edited by Gudrun Höy. Story editing by Bobi Martin

Enchanté Publishing
P.O. Box 620471, Woodside, CA 94062

Printed in Singapore

Library of Congress Cataloging-in-Publication Data
Farrington, Liz.
Tanya and the green-eyed monster/story created by Liz Farrington,
written by Jonathan Sherwood; illustrated by Jeremy Thornton. — 2nd ed.
          p.   cm.
Summary: Tanya's jealousy of her sister becomes a monster which she
is able to tame through the use of magic paints.
ISBN 1-56844-102-9
[1. Jealousy - Fiction. 2. Sibling rivalry - Fiction 3. Sisters - Fiction
4. Monsters - Fiction]
I. Sherwood, Jonathan. II. Thornton, Jeremy, ill. III. Title.
PZF.F24618Tan   1995   (E)—dc20   95-36447

Second Edition
10 9 8 7 6 5 4 3 2 1

Tanya and the Green-Eyed Monster

Story created by Liz Farrington
Written by Jonathan Sherwood
Illustrated by Jeremy Thornton

Enchanté Publishing

Tanya rushed in for lunch letting the screen door bang behind her.

"Don't slam the door," said her mother. "How did you get leaves in your hair already?"

"I was in my treehouse," Tanya said.

"Why can't you stay clean, like your sister?" her mother asked with a sigh.

Tanya glared at her little sister. "We can't all be like Little Miss Perfect," she said sarcastically.

"That was uncalled for!" snapped her mother. "Go brush your hair, and see if you can do something with your attitude while you're at it."

Tanya stormed into her room. She slammed the door and then kicked it. *Too bad it wasn't Jenny's head,* she fumed.

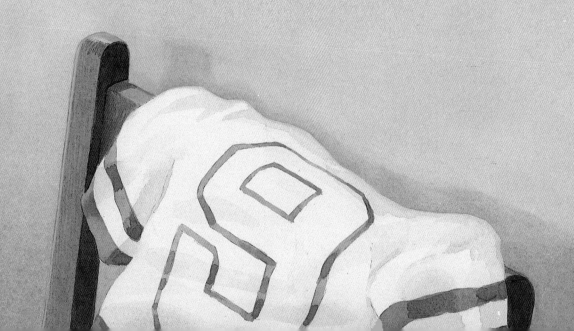

A few minutes later Jenny knocked on Tanya's door.
"Mom says lunch is ready, Tanya."

"Get lost!"

"We're having pizza," Jenny said softly.

Tanya ran a brush through her hair and washed her hands.
When she got to the table, her mother was cutting Jenny's pizza
into bite-size pieces. Jenny frowned, but said nothing. Tanya
smiled as she scraped the topping off her pizza and stuffed the crust into her mouth.

"What are you doing, Tanya?" asked her father.

"I like to eat the crust first and then the topping," Tanya said as she took another big bite.

"Why can't you eat neatly, like your sister?" he asked.

Tanya flung her pizza onto her plate. "Jenny, Jenny, Jenny!" She slammed her fist against
the table. "That's all you two ever think about!" She ran to her room.

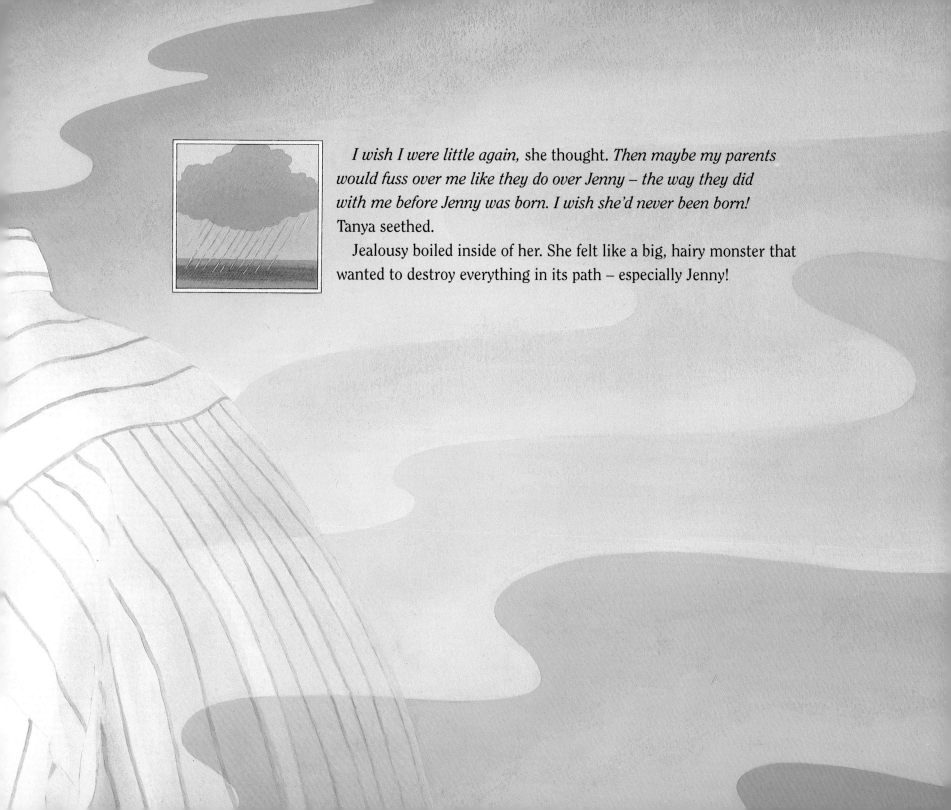

I wish I were little again, she thought. *Then maybe my parents would fuss over me like they do over Jenny – the way they did with me before Jenny was born. I wish she'd never been born!* Tanya seethed.

Jealousy boiled inside of her. She felt like a big, hairy monster that wanted to destroy everything in its path – especially Jenny!

Tanya slipped quietly out of the house and climbed up to her treehouse. She was sitting there, feeling miserable, when suddenly she saw rainbow-colored beams of light pouring down from a tree out in the field. Fascinated, Tanya climbed down and ran out to the big tree. She jumped from one beam of light to the next. When she got to the last one, she was surprised to find a door in the side of the tree. More rainbow lights sparkled inside.

Tanya peeked through the door. "Hello, Tanya," said a warm voice. "I'm so glad you've come."

"How did you know my name?" Tanya asked. "Who are you?"

"I'm Mrs. Murgatroyd," said the woman. "I know the names of all the children who need my magical paints. Would you like to paint something?"

Tanya nodded. She couldn't take her eyes off the shimmering rainbow colors as they flowed into their special pots.

"The rainbows give the paints their magic," Mrs. Murgatroyd said as she set paints and paper on the table. "Everything you paint can be changed with a stroke of your brush."

Tanya had meant to paint a picture of herself, but to her surprise she painted a huge monster with big, green eyes. As she looked at her picture, the monster glared at her. One hand reached up out of the paper. Tanya started to scream, then remembered what Mrs. Murgatroyd had said.

Quickly she painted strong bars to cage the monster. As she painted the last bar, the monster vanished from the picture.

"What's happening?" Tanya asked in surprise. She looked
up at Mrs. Murgatroyd.

"A jealous monster seems scary when it's locked up inside
of you," Mrs. Murgatroyd told her. She led Tanya to the door.
Tanya could see the monster hiding behind a bush.
He did not seem so scary now. "Go talk to your monster, Tanya."

As Tanya started walking across the clearing, the monster ran to hide behind
a big tree. Each time she got close, it ran and hid again.

When Tanya caught up to her monster she was surprised to see lots of other monsters there, too. And people! Friends from school were there, and so were her parents. Even Jenny was there! Some people were talking to their monsters quietly, and some were having a hard time trying to get them under control.

Did everyone have a jealous monster?

A boy she knew from school had put a leash on his monster.
As he began to talk to the monster Tanya could see it shrink in size.
Her monster was huge. Tanya took a deep breath. *I can do that too,*
she thought.

She turned to her monster and began to talk to it. With each
sentence it seemed to grow a little quieter, a little smaller.

After a while she put a collar and leash on her monster like some of the others had done. A few people with well-behaved monsters were giving lessons on how to be in charge of them. Tanya watched and tried to learn from them. Sure enough, her monster did get a little smaller.

Over a loudspeaker an announcer invited people to enter some competitions with their monsters. There were all kinds of contests – some for jumping, some for running, some for drawing and some for singing. Every monster won first place at something! Tanya's monster won first place at the tree-climbing contest.

"I wish I knew how to climb a tree," said Jenny.

Tanya looked at her sister in surprise. "I thought you just liked playing with your dolls."

"I always wanted to play in the treehouse you built," she said quietly, "but I was afraid Mom would get mad if I got dirty. You get to do all the fun stuff."

Is that why Jenny has a jealous monster? Tanya wondered.

"Come on, Jenny," Tanya said. "I'll show you how I learned to climb trees."

Later they watched from a tree branch as Jenny's monster won first place in the joke-telling contest. By the end of the day, the two monsters were no bigger than one of Jenny's dolls.

"Hey, I did it!" Jenny exclaimed with glee.

Tanya was startled to find herself back in her own treehouse. She stared at Jenny in amazement. "What are you doing up here?" she asked.

"Mom told me to call you for dinner," Jenny said. "And well, I always wanted to climb up here, but I didn't think I could. Are you still mad?"

To her surprise, Tanya found she wasn't. "Come on, Jenny," she said,
"I'll help you climb down, and tomorrow we can do something up here together."
"Thanks, Tanya!" Jenny squealed with delight.
"What's for dinner?" Tanya asked as they started up the path.
"Fried chicken, your favorite!" Jenny giggled.